SPLENDOUR BOOKS

XXII

PHOTOTYPESET IN ENGLAND BY BAS PRINTERS LIMITED, WALLOP
MADE AND PRINTED IN ITALY BY FRATELLI FABBRI EDITORI, MILAN,
FOR THE PUBLISHERS, W. H. ALLEN AND CO., ESSEX STREET, LONDON, WC2.
PUBLISHED IN AUSTRALIA BY GOLDEN PRESS PTY. LTD., SYDNEY
© FRATELLI FABBRI EDITORI 1966

TALES FROM AUSTRALIA

Retold by Shirley Goulden

Illustrated by Benvenuti

W. H. Allen

CONTENTS

TALE OF THE FLOWERS

There were stories told in Australia, long before the white man ever came there – tales of imaginary folk who inhabited the heavens and earth. The little Aboriginals heard the stories from their parents, and in time had little Aboriginals of their own to tell them to. And the stories, like the gods they depicted, lived for ever, so that children all over the world could enjoy them. Some went rather like this:

There was a wise man – his name was Baiame – and, in the pursuit of life's secrets, he became old. At length the venerable head bowed under the weight of such great wisdom, and the old man decided he was world weary, and must retire to the restful heavens. But the earth was sad to lose one of its greatest prophets, and when he had gone, all the flowers bowed their heads too. One by one they shrivelled and died, and the land was barren and lonely. Even the industrious bees took themselves and their honey away, for there was no work. It seemed to the people that Baiame had taken the very sweetness of life with him, when he had gone away to the heavens.

As the years passed there was hardly a soul left who remembered the bright beauty of flowers, the delicacy of their scent. And there was not a child who had savoured the dulcet taste of golden honey. Babies

5

cried for it, fathers searched for it, and mothers even tried to make it —
but of course they couldn't. With all the colour and sweetness gone
out of their lives, everyone became drab, cheerless, thoroughly out
of sorts.

It was the gloominess of his friends and neighbours that had driven
Neki, an undistinguished member of the tribe, from home. Even the
kangaroos on the plains were better company than some he knew,
thought Neki, who had gone much farther than he intended. At night-
fall there was nothing for it but to make a bed for himself among the
bushes, at a careful distance from the river, which contained some
unfriendly crocodiles.

Neki went to sleep among the bushes, near the crocodile river; but
he awoke to the warm buzzing of bees. The air was deep scented by
a glorious mass of flowers, whose colourful splendour so dazzled Neki
that he was obliged to close his eyes tight again. When he opened
them, wonder of wonders, the flowers and the bees were still there!
No doubt about it, he must have been transported straight to the

heavens, for such happy sights as this had long since vanished from the earth.

Neki sprang up, longing to embrace the lovely blooms, to suck from the flowers their delicious honey, to know at last the very sweetness of life itself. But as his arm stretched out to grasp what he had so long desired, a voice from nowhere, and at the same time from everywhere around, cried: "Touch not what is not yours to touch. These are the flowers of Baiame, whom the gods favour."

Neki knew better than to anger the gods, though it was hard enough not to at that moment. Dutifully however he fell on his knees, forehead to the ground, and waited to hear what he *might* do.

"Rise," ordered the voice, in kindlier tones. "I can see you have respect for the property of others."

Neki stood up, somewhat shakily. "Permit me to ask," he said to the thin air around him, "permit me to ask if I am in the heavens, or on the earth?"

"Heavens?" The voice sounded scornful. "You, a creature of no

consequence, imagine yourself to be with the gods? Young people think well of themselves these days, to be sure!''

From this Neki gathered that he was still in the land of mortals – but what a changed land it was! How happy his tribe would be – and how grateful to his humble self, who had discovered the flowers again. But the voice did not propose to allow Neki to take undeserved credit.

"Know now that these flowers are sent to you by the generosity of wise Baiame. He has beseeched the gods, in the name of your people, to return to their sight the great gift of beauty. They are yours to dazzle the eye and delight the senses. Yet remember that loveliness is but an image in the mind of man. Touch these flowers and they will shrivel and fade; for beauty is not given but lent to the earth. And surely if man reach out to possess it, that beauty shall pass away.''

All of which meant very much the same as the sign you must have seen (and obeyed of course) in the park – "Please Keep Off the Grass". Neki had never been to a park, but nevertheless he understood well enough that the flowers were not, on any account, to be picked.

"As I stand before you, O voice from the heavens, I swear that I shall defend, with my spear and with my life, the property of the wise Baiame,'' said Neki.

"Well spoken,'' the voice observed. "And may you have strength to keep this vow. Now return to your people with good tidings.''

Neki stopped neither for rest nor refreshment, but made his way directly back to the village.

"My people, I am come among you from a place where can be seen a great wonder!'' he cried. The villagers gathered around him curiously.

"What wonder is shown to such a lowly one as you, that shall be hidden from the eyes of his betters?'' demanded the chief's son. He

8

was much the same age as Neki, but considered himself, according to his birth, very superior.

"Wonders of wonders!" replied Neki. "The wise man Baiame has induced the gods to send us a magnificent gift. Hear me, for I say that the flowers and bees have returned to the earth!"

The children stared, round-eyed. "Flowers, bees, what are they? Shall we be able to play with them?"

"Flowers?" gasped the wives and mothers. "Our great great grandmothers heard tell of such. More beautiful than the sunshine – they brought colour and life to the world, it was said."

"Bees, you speak of?" asked the young and old men. "Are they not servants of the gods, they who carry their food of great sweetness and delight, called 'honey'? Yet you, unimportant one, speak of such marvels as we have never hoped to enjoy?"

"It is I who bring you this news," said Neki. "I, of small account, who am honoured to be messenger of the gods themselves!"

Dubious as they were, the villagers began to believe what Neki had proclaimed; for it is far easier to accept good news than bad. Even the chief's son was prepared to accompany Neki to the place where the flowers had been, in the hope perhaps that the young man might be discredited.

All but the very young and the very old made ready for the journey across the plains, led by Neki, who felt himself a god among men for once. After a day and a night they came to the place where Neki had heard the voice, and sure enough the fragrant scent of flowers greeted them. Suddenly life was no longer drab and dull, but filled with radiance and colour, brightness and hope.

"Be praised!" cried everyone, old and young alike. "Be praised, for beauty has returned in our time!" Men, women and children fell on their knees and touched foreheads in the dust – except for the chief's

son, whose pride would not allow him to give thanks for the great gift they had received. But in a moment lowered eyes were lifted longingly towards the glowing flowers, yearning fingers stretched forth towards the source of the honey.

"Let us pluck the flowers which Baiame has sent to us. Let us plant their seeds in our own land beyond the plain. Let us make the flowers live forever to grace our tribe." And: "Let us eat of the honey," cried the children. "Let us eat our fill of the good food that Baiame has given. For never in all our lives have we tasted that which is sweet."

"Let us take all for ourselves!" shouted the chief's son, and jumped forward.

That was the moment when Neki proved himself nobler by nature than he was by birth. Had he not been chosen by the gods themselves to protect the gifts of Baiame? Flinging his arms wide, he stood between his people and the precious flowers, bravely stopping their way.

"Stand aside!" the chief's son shouted angrily.

"Son of our chief, neither you, nor any man, shall steal these heavenly gifts," said Neki. "Be glad that the earth contains such glory, and let it be!"

The people were silent.

The chief's son raised his spear ready to strike down Neki for his temerity; and the others, who would have taken what was not theirs, muttered encouragement. But the spear was flung from the young man's grasp by the chief himself.

"What evil is this, my son?" he demanded in horror. "Would you bring the displeasure of the gods upon our tribe? For it is clearly forbidden, even as the young man maintains, to touch the gifts of Baiame!" The other elders, wise in their old age, nodded in agreement. "The gods must be respected," they said. "No one shall touch the gifts of Baiame."

Then the chief commanded all to return to their village, while he and the elders prepared to keep guard, day and night, over the flowers. Even his son dared not disobey such an order, though he slunk away with ill grace.

The village seemed more bare and colourless than ever, in contrast to the flowers beyond the plain. And the souls of the people became starved for beauty; their eyes grew as dull and faded as the barren land. "Give us some flowers!" they beseeched the dried and yellow bushes. "We yearn for the flowers!"

"Give us some honey," cried the children to the flies droning on the rubbish heaps. But the flies could not

make honey like the musical bees, however hard they tried. "Go to your father," said the people to the chief's son. "Go and beg that we shall have honey for our children; for if you do not, the children will grow sick from crying." The chief's son did not dare confront his father with such a demand, but he sent his wife instead, bearing a wooden bowl. She walked for a night and a day, and at last arrived at the place beyond the plain, where the flowers grew.

The elders sat in a silent group, warily guarding the gift of Baiame. The woman bowed before them. "I have been sent, wise fathers, to

inform you that our tribe fares sorrowfully since the gifts of Baiame have been sent to the earth. For to have, and yet to have not is unendurable to our suffering people. Permit us to take only one bowl full of honey so that our children may, once in their lives, taste of its sweetness." But the chief and the elders were adamant.

"Go back to the tribe, woman, and bid them forget that ever they saw the delicacy of the flowers yielding to the perfumed breeze, or heard the busy song of the bees spinning their golden thread. For it is not permitted to take of the gift of Baiame. So we have said, and thus shall it be. For to anger the gods is to bring woe to our people. Tell my son, who has sent you, that he must hear the wisdom of his father. For have I not lived his life thrice over and thought his thoughts?" So the woman wearily went back to the village, bearing an empty bowl; and there was much wailing from those who greeted her.

Matters had reached a sorry pass and it seemed that the tribe could not survive much longer without a little sweetness in their lives. Not only the children, but their parents too began to grow weak with craving for the gifts of the gods.

Neki could not bear to see his people suffering in this way. He felt responsible for their disappointment,

having been the first to discover the sacred place where flowers grew and honey flowed. If they had not seen these wondrous things, perhaps now the people might not yearn for them so? Neki came to a momentous decision. He would go himself to Baiame, there in the heavens, and beseech him to help them. "Go to the heavens?" The villagers were aghast. Who but the gods knows how to get there?"

But Neki had always been a wanderer. Had he not travelled the plains from corner to corner, even up to the foot of the Oobi Oobi mountain? And it was this mountain which stretched so high that it

touched the clouds themselves. Surely, thought Neki, if he could climb to the top of the mountain, he would come at last to the heavens where the venerable Baiame rested?

"The way is far. You will never come back alive," said the chief's son, who wished he had courage enough to go himself.

"Then I shall lose my life in a worthy cause," replied Neki stoutly. "But I believe that the gods are good, and that they will return me safely to my people. Only promise that you will not touch the sacred flowers until I come back." The people made him a solemn vow that

no matter how strong grew their craving, they would never go beyond the plain, even to look again upon the heavenly gifts, until Neki came home.

Neki prepared for his journey, then departed from his village alone and unarmed. Even the trusty boomerang that he used for hunting was left behind. For he went on a mission of peace, to a place where no man needed to defend himself. And the people were saddened to see him go, for no one thought they would ever set eyes on the young man again.

The journey to the Oobi Oobi mountain took many days, and Neki was sore of foot and tired when he came in sight of the towering peaks. How tall and inaccessible the mountain seemed! The lower reaches were almost as smooth as a pumice-stone, with never a safe foothold or a jutting crag which Neki could grasp to haul himself upward.

Neki made his way round the mountain, hopefully seeking a path, and at last he found one – a narrow straggling passageway falling away steeply on one side. Dropping on all fours like a monkey, Neki felt his way cautiously along the path, trying not to look downwards at the sheer drop which fell away at his side at increasing distances. Higher and higher he climbed, until as the light began to wane, the path stopped abruptly at the foot of some high steps carved in the rock. The stairs seemed to stretch upwards unendingly, through the clouds themselves, and Neki, thoroughly exhausted, fell before them in a deep sleep. When he awoke the sun was shining, turning the rocky stairs into a golden way. So Neki, full of renewed vigour, began to climb upwards, high towards the heavens.

On the way he found bushes heavy with luscious berries to sustain him, and here and there a spring of fresh water sparkled down the mountainside. As Neki ate and drank, he felt full of hope, courage and determination to reach the summit. It seemed that the gods were with him on this tremendous undertaking. Truly he was born to be a leader of men, more surely than was the son of the chief!

Upwards and onwards, scrambling over stones, leaping narrow gullies where the stairs gaped, regaining his unsteady balance, and climbing the next and the next and the next step, Neki went higher.

And where the peak of the mountain tipped the vaporous cloud, Neki passed out of the sunlight into the cool clear light of the morning star.

"Neki," called a voice – and he knew it was the voice from beyond the plains. "What brings you here to the heavens, boy?" Neki fell to his knees. "O voice, whoever you are – permit me to speak to the wise Baiame."

"You have come far and endured much, to that end," the voice went on. "For what pressing reason should you wish to speak to Baiame? Perhaps to seek yet another favour?"

"A favour indeed, though not for myself," replied Neki. "I beg that the wise Baiame will grant my people the right to possess the flowers

and the honey from the bees, which he has so graciously lent to the earth. For there is no colour nor sweetness in their lives, and they are indeed sorrowful."

In the clear light one of the drifting clouds seemed to assume the shape of an old man, with a long smoky beard, who held up his arm, pointing towards the north. "That which you ask shall be granted," said the voice, and it came from the drifting cloud. "For I am he whom you seek, Baiame. Go back to your people and tell them that, as a reward for their honesty and restraint in protecting what is mine, what is mine shall for ever more be theirs!"

Now the ground began to rumble and tumble and shake and swell. Neki watched in startled astonishment as rivulets of tiny cracks appeared – widening, as small colourful heads pushed insistently upwards and outwards through the rocky surface. The heads were the heads of plants, and as they rose, the buds and leaves uncurled in all their magnificence. The ground was a mass of glorious colour – flowers

shot up even between Neki's toes – and the scent was intoxicating. Neki was overcome by the sudden blaze of glory, and fell down flat on his face among the heavenly blooms.

"Take the flowers, for they are yours," intoned the voice from the cloud, which Neki now knew to belong to Baiame himself. As he lifted his head again, the misty cloud dissolved into a shower of sparkling rain which fell like gurgling laughter all about him.

Gathering great armfuls of the exotic plants, Neki retraced his steps down the mountain. The rigours of the journey seemed washed away by the rain, and light in foot and spirit the young man returned to his village.

The wonder of the people knew no limit, when Neki appeared to tell his astonishing tale. With what care the plants were put in the ground and watered and tended – with what joy were the elders brought back to their village, which was suddenly alive with light and sunshine. And how merry were the children when the bees came

buzzing round the flowers, for they knew that life would be sweet at last.

Neki was much honoured by his people – even by the chief's son who no longer bore enmity towards him. The chief made Neki a leader of the tribe, and in time he became wise and respected like the great Baiame. And when he grew old, and the time came for him to go once more to the heavens, the gods welcomed him with open arms. And there were flowers all the way.

TALE OF THE MOON

Long ago, when the nights were so dark that no one went out after sundown, there lived a hunter of possums called Wapiti. That is, *he* considered himself a hunter, but the possums did not. The cunning little creatures always managed to elude him, and poor Wapiti never captured a single one.

"Here strides Wapiti, the great hunter!" jeered the men of his village, when he returned possumless and discouraged from his daily expeditions. And to hide his humiliation Wapiti would brag a little. "Tomorrow I shall catch more possums than any of you have ever seen. Yes, I, Wapiti, the mightiest hunter in all the village. Tomorrow – only wait until tomorrow!" But when tomorrow became today, Wapiti still came back with an empty sack. "We wait, mighty hunter!" mocked Mumba, who could hunt the kangaroo as well as the possum. "Make haste with your large catch, so that we may see it before our eyes grow dim with age!"

Once Wapiti was so stung by the scorn of his friends that he made a most extravagant claim. "Hear you, Mumba – you who are renowned for your skill in the light of day! Wapiti shall become a hunter of the night!" This new boast was greeted with howls of derision.

"These are idle words," Mumba exclaimed. "That he who has caught nothing during the day, would hardly venture out into the darkness. The sun shall never go down on such a night, my friends!"

"The sun goes now, and I go too!" cried Wapiti wildly. "We shall soon discover who is the better man, Mumba." To the astonishment of everyone – including himself – Wapiti really did set out to save his reputation, in the very black of night.

However there were no possums to be seen, or anything else for that matter, in the forest. As Wapiti stumbled from tree to tree in the dark, he wished most heartily that he had not laid claim to such an undertaking. He would very likely have to stay in the forest until daybreak, and return, as usual, to the village empty-handed, only to be tormented anew.

Then, unexpectedly, his foot caught in a tangled root, and Wapiti fell flat on his face. He was too discouraged to move for a moment, and lay there with his head in his hands. Was it his imagination or did a tiny crack of light show through his outstretched fingers? How strange, for everyone knew that the sun, which had set long ago, was the only source of light. Scrambling to his knees, Wapiti looked closely at the ground, and discovered there was indeed a narrow glowing light, coming from a fissure in the earth. Thoroughly curious, Wapiti began to pull up the earth, until he had made a hole large enough for him to scramble through. Feet first, Wapiti fell into a

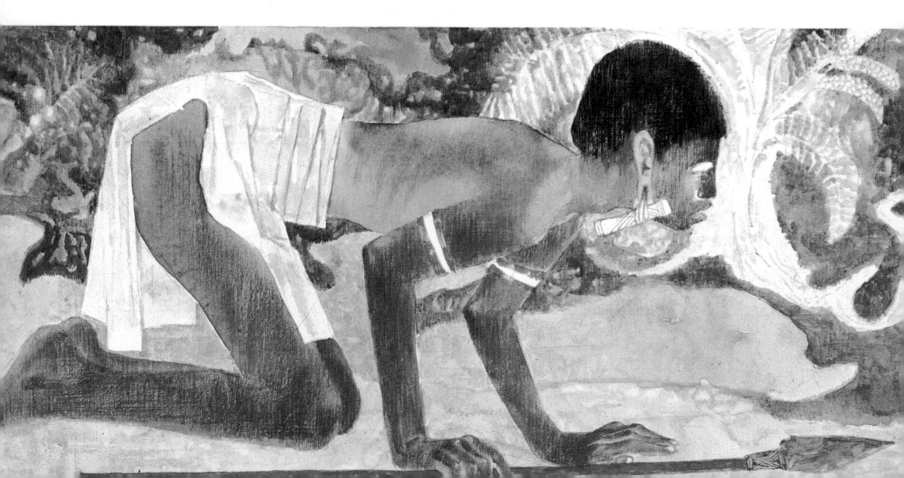

narrow cavern, lit with a cool, unearthly light. Crossing the cave, he came to yet a larger one, and there in the centre, surrounded by a ring of stones, lay a spear and shield. Guarding his eyes with a hand, for the light had grown blindingly strong, Wapiti saw that the light was coming from a brilliant disk set into the shield. Here indeed was an unusual discovery! Such a spear and shield could have no ordinary merit, and Wapiti longed to possess them. But to whom did they belong? Perhaps to some magician, who would turn him into a possum, only to be captured by his rival Mumba. Wapiti decided to make sure that the shield and the spear were his for the taking.

Going back to the smaller cavern, where the light was not quite so intense, Wapiti sat under the hole through which he had entered.

He waited and waited and waited for the appearance, natural or otherwise, of the owner of the spear and shield. But nobody came. As the sun rose above the hole where he sat, the strange silver light that had come from the shield, gradually faded and then died out altogether. Wapiti advanced cautiously into the second cavern again and examined the shield. It was quite dim in the cave now that the shield no longer shed an unearthly glow. Indeed it now appeared to be quite an ordinary object, with a white painted circle in the centre. The spear too, at close quarters, seemed exactly like any other spear, and Wapiti began to wonder if after all his discovery was as important as he had thought it. He might as well take the things away, for they seemed to be the sort of shield and spear that any of the village men could make in a few hours.

So, armed with the spear, and with the shield over his shoulder, Wapiti went to the outer cavern, where the hole gaped above his head. But how could he climb out? The hole was high, and there was no foothold in the rock. It was then that Wapiti proved himself as nimble a huntsman as ever wielded a spear. He ran forward, dug the spear in the ground, and used it to vault vigorously upwards and out through the hole. Once above ground it was simple work to lean back into the cave, stretch out his arm, grasp the head of the spear and pull it towards him.

Wapiti hoped that his new spear and shield would bring him good fortune, and he set off after the elusive possum. But alas, the wily creatures had no intention of being caught, and ran away faster than he could chase. It was dusk again, and Wapiti was no nearer to redeeming his reputation than before. As the sun faded away, leaving the forest in stifling darkness, Wapiti propped himself against a tree, much dispirited. No matter how hard he tried, it seemed he would never become a mighty huntsman. Could it be that the contempt of Mumba and his friends was justified? Never would he return to his village again to suffer more ridicule!

All at once the gloom was pierced by a clear light, throwing the trees and their fine tracery of leaves into stark white clarity. Wapiti stood transfixed by the beauty of the scene. The white disk on the shield had begun to send forth powerful silver rays, just as it had done in the cavern beneath the ground. Now Wapiti knew he had indeed found something far more wonderful than he realized, for this shield was a treasure beyond treasures! And suddenly its magical powers were evident. For along the diamond-bright pathways of the forest came possum after possum, their cunning little eyes gleaming with the desire to bathe in that beautiful cool light. Nearer and nearer to the glowing shield they trooped, and Wapiti, overcoming his astonishment, hastily opened his large sack and placed it near the shield. As they came closer the strong beam dazzled the possums and they walked unresistingly into the sack. Quite exhausted by his triumph and by the hard brightness of the light, Wapiti fastened the neck of his sack tightly and imprisoned the possums inside. Then he settled down to sleep until daybreak.

In the morning the mighty hunter hid the shield and the spear and returned to his village, with the largest sackful of possum ever seen in those parts. The same people who had derided him now showered Wapiti with fulsome praise. Truly he was a man among men, and champion of all huntsmen!

Only Mumba refused to believe that Wapiti had made this

enormous catch without the aid of some mysterious power. During the feast held that night in Wapiti's honour, Mumba could not bring himself to eat a morsel. "Hail Wapiti, mighty hunter of darkness!" cried the villagers. And Mumba glowered, silently promising that they should know Wapiti better before the dawn of next day.

When the celebrations were over, to the music of admiring cheers, Wapiti went off hunting again. Behind him, in the diminishing dusk, crept Mumba. As the black night closed in, Wapiti made haste to the place where he had left his precious possessions – the spear and shield – and Mumba followed softly behind. Concealed by a large tree he watched as Wapiti took up his spear and shield. What magic was this? Mumba saw that from the shield a great silvery ray lit up the forest in brilliant relief. Then he saw groups of possum moving towards the source of light, and into the sack which Wapiti held out to receive them. "Cheat, impostor!" yelled Mumba, and charging furiously from his hiding place he snatched up the wonderful shield, and made off with it into the forest. Wapiti dropped the sack in shock, and, regardless of the escaping possums, ran after Mumba, guided by the light from the shield. Mumba was a fast runner, but the possums, in fear of their lives, ran faster. Under his feet they scuttled, and both the shield and Mumba fell. Wapiti caught up with him and furiously

grabbed the shield. "Thief in the night!" he shouted.

"You, you are the thief!" gasped Mumba. "Who gave you the right to such a marvel? Where did you find it – tell me that?" Wapiti's rage began to turn into uncomfortable shame. He knew that the shield was no more his than Mumba's. "You speak justly," he said. "This wondrous creation is meant not for one man but for many. Indeed I believe it to be a gift of the gods."

"Well spoken!" replied Mumba. "Let us then agree to return it to where it rightly belongs. Dealing the shield a mighty kick he sent it streaking in a brilliant pathway of light, up to the heavens. The round white disk jumped out of the shield and fixed itself firmly in the skies. And from then onwards the nights were lit by that silvery glow, which men call the moon.

TALE OF THE FIRE

There was a time before fire came to the earth, when there lived a disagreeable old man called Wedewede. Day in, day out, Wedewede never stopped complaining: "Not a wink of sleep had I all night," he announced every morning. "Woe is me, for the lot of an old man is hard. Where shall he find a few warm skins to cover his aching bones?" And when his granddaughter, Warbol, who was married to a trapper, gave him her own kangaroo sleeping-bag, Wedewede only moaned louder the next day.

"Not a wink of sleep had I all night" he declared. "For what benefit is a pair of warm feet to a stomach aching with hunger? Woe, woe is me, for who can be expected to provide food for an old man who has grown too feeble to hunt?" The trapper had made a good haul, so Warbol gave the old man a fine piece of fresh meat for his supper. Yet no word of thanks did she receive. Instead, the following morning: "Not a wink of sleep had I all night," groaned Wedewede. "For without teeth, how can a poor creature hope to chew raw meat? Woe, woe, woe is me, for who shall mourn an old man's passing, for want of a decent meal?" At this even the kind Warbol lost patience. "Get away from here, old man, for there is no way of pleasing such a

31

miserable creature – no way in the wide world!"

"Woe, woe, woe, woe!" Wedewede was sorrier for himself than ever. "Nobody wants an old body like me, not even my own flesh and blood. I shall go away; for in this place there is no respect for the aged. Perhaps, my girl, you will then mourn your old grandfather, who never caused anyone a moment's care in all his seventy years."

"And never did a day's work, either, in all those years," replied Warbol, quite exasperated. But she regretted her impatience, for the old man really had taken offence, and left the village, stiff with outraged dignity. "Woe, woe, woe, woe, woe," he wailed, as he went on his way. "Not a soul anywhere to care if an old man lives or dies!"

However Wedewede was not as helpless as he pretended to be. Away from the village he managed to live well enough by his own efforts, eating fruit for the most part, and drinking fresh spring water. But he was far from happy nevertheless; for who in the wide forest could lend an ear to his tales of misfortune?  "Woe, woe, woe, woe, woe," he cried, rubbing two pieces of stone together, in anguish. "Pity the lot of an old man who receives no sympathy!" Suddenly Wedewede became more woeful than ever, for the flints he had been rubbing together struck a spark and burned his hand. The spark fell on some dry leaves, which immediately caught fire. Wedewede regarded the flames in amazement, for no such sight had yet been seen on earth. Thoughtfully he added some pieces of wood to the fire, and found that his old bones were quite eased by the warm glow that spread towards him. Earlier in the day he had managed to catch a possum, and this he now skinned, and placed on a stick over the bright flames.

The delicious odour of cooking for the first time provoked the appetite of man. Even toothless Wedewede had no difficulty in eating the cooked possum with great enjoyment.

That night, the first in many a year, Wedewede slept content – his feet warm in the glow of the fire, and a good meal inside him. In the morning he awoke feeling fifty years young, and in a cheerful mood! Burying the flints in the ground beneath a certain rock, he made his way back to the village, full of glee.

"They who sent an old man forth to fare for himself shall find him well able to do so," he chuckled. "But the cosy secret shall be mine alone. They shall not profit who did not profit me!" Thus, in an uncharitable frame of mind, he greeted his granddaughter who had always been so kind and generous to him.

In the next few days Warbol feared that her grandfather's absence from the village had caused his mind to wander too. For instead of eating the food she provided, the old man would take it away to some secret place in the forest. To whom was he taking the food, and would he not himself die of starvation? Warbol, who was fond of her grand-

father, in spite of his irritating ways, felt most concerned. One day she decided to follow him into the forest. Taking a bowl of food with her, in case she should discover that her grandfather had indeed given all his away and was hungry, Warbol kept her distance behind him, until they were some way into the woods. Then it was that something occurred which caused Warbol to lose sight of the old man. Two birds stood in her path, a yellow and an orange cockatoo. They opened their beaks wide, crying: "Food, food, food!"

"Poor creatures," exclaimed the good-natured Warbol. "They seem in greater need than my grandfather." So she gave the birds her bowl of food. They gobbled it up and flew away in a flash of orange and yellow flame.

Now Warbol began to seek her grandfather in the forest, and seeing a strange white cloud billowing up above the trees, she followed it. Through a gap in the undergrowth Warbol was amazed to see a great, crackling, smoking pile of

wood, from which rose the most desirable smell of roasting possum. Old Wedewede was leaning over the fire, intent in savouring the aroma of the cooking. He nearly jumped as far out of his skin as the unfortunate possum, when Warbol spoke. "What marvel is this, grandfather? Such light and heat, warmer even than the rays of the sun!" Wedewede bounded up in a perfect fury. "Woe, woe, woe, woe, woe, woe, WOE!" he shrieked. "That a girl should spy upon her own grandfather!"

"But I followed only to see that all was well with you, grandfather," said Warbol. "And so I find you, well enough indeed. For this miracle you have found will surely be of great comfort to our tribe. Our children shall no longer suffer the cold, and our men shall eat food which will warm them inside. Then they will grow more strong and brave, and able to provide for us more plentifully."

The selfish old man had no intention

of sharing his good fortune with anyone, however.

"It is mine, this warmth, this comfort. Mine alone. And no man save I shall know of it!" he cried. "Mark this, granddaughter, I forbid you to speak of my secret to anyone." Warbol made no reply. She squatted down opposite her grandfather, staring fascinated at the darting flames. Wedewede, mistaking her silence for submission, finished his meal of possum and settled down for a contented nap. But Warbol pondered on the wonders of this new miracle, and how it could change all of their lives for the better. Her grandfather should not be allowed to keep this benefit to himself alone. It belonged to all men, and she, Warbol, intended to see that they received it. Careful not to disturb the old man, she reached over and gently withdrew one of the burning sticks from the fire. Holding the flickering flame cautiously, she retraced her footsteps towards the village. Unfortunately, however, Warbol had disturbed the fire, which went out. Wedewede, feeling chilled, awoke to find his granddaughter gone, and set off in angry pursuit. He could see the light from Warbol's fire-stick, weaving in and out of the trees, and moving surprisingly nimbly for an old man who claimed to have aching bones, he hurried after her. "Woe, woe, woe, woe, woe, woe, WOE, WOE!" he shrilled. "My granddaughter has stolen my secret from me, and wants to give it to those who don't deserve it! She shall suffer for this when I lay hold of her – scheming, traitorous female!" His sentiments were no more charitable towards his granddaughter than they had been before he left her.

Warbol, not knowing that her grandfather was close behind, walked slowly, bearing her precious flame which must not go out until it had lit a great bonfire of branches that her people could keep alight for ever. So the poor girl received a terrible fright when the old man suddenly darted out at her from behind a bush and yelled: "Miserable

stealer of miracles, I have caught you! Now prepare to pay for your shameful treatment of a helpless old man!" Plucking some twigs, Wedewede, quite beside himself with rage, was about to set upon Warbol and administer a beating, when two cockatoos – one yellow and one orange – flew down from a tree between the two of them.

"Help me and my people!" begged Warbol. "Let not this warmth be extinguished before it reaches those who need it!" The birds opened their beaks and squawked: "Water, water, water!" At once a widening stream appeared between the old man and his grand-daughter. Wedewede was obliged to jump back hastily.

"My thanks, and the thanks of my people!" called Warbol, as she continued on her way, leaving the frenzied Wedewede dancing up and down helplessly on the opposite bank of the stream. Now the old man's anger was uncontrolled. With the strength that only fury and desperation could lend him, he plucked a small tree from the earth, hurled it into the stream – and himself astride it. The tree floated its

irate passenger to the opposite bank, and Wedewede was off hot-foot and hot-head after his granddaughter. Warbol, thinking she had left Wedewede safely on the other side of the stream, picked her way slowly through the undergrowth, still holding the burning stick.

The old man soon came up with Warbol again, and dashing out at her from behind a tree, he snatched the stick out of her grasp and beat out the flame. "Now the secret is mine for ever," he shouted. "And no person on this earth shall ever learn from me the way to light up this stick again. I alone shall enjoy the warmth of its glow, the aroma of roasting food. The luxuries of life are for me, and no one shall share them!" Warbol stared in dismay at the blackened smoking stick. The fire was out, and only her grandfather knew the way to light it.

But now the flame had gone out, it seemed that her grandfather's anger had died too. Perhaps the fire had struck a small spark of sympathy in his heart? Now he saw how crestfallen his granddaughter appeared, and he began to think of the many kindnesses she had bestowed upon him. He felt ashamed. "See here, granddaughter, I shall make one more flame, if you wish it so dearly," he said, and picking up a pair of flints, Wedewede tried to make another fire. But try as he did, the fire would not light. "Assuredly the gods have punished me for my greed," he moaned. "It was I who first discovered the gods' secret, and now it is to be denied me. Woe, woe and a thousand woes that the gods should thus chastise a miserable old sinner."

"Come grandfather, I forgive you at any rate," said Warbol, generous as ever. "Let us return home and try to be more contented with our lot as it is, even without the miracle." For once Wedewede made no complaint, and meekly followed his granddaughter back to the village. They were met on the outskirts by the two cockatoos, who had flown there before them. Opening their beaks they cried: "Fire, fire, fire!" And taking wing again, the birds swept upwards towards the trees, in a yellow and orange arc. As they passed, the wings of the birds gently tipped a huge bush that grew alone in a clearing. And the bush burst into a large circle of yellow and orange flame. From then on the bush was never allowed to go out, until the day came, many years later, when men learned how to make fire for themselves.

TALE OF THE RAINBOW

From beyond the setting sun, where the plains met with the sky, there appeared among the Garadjari tribe a strange pair. Two sisters they called themselves, one old and ugly, the other young and pleasing. The elder sister firmly announced her intention of remaining with the tribe, and set down her heavy basket in the nearest convenient hut. The younger sister, who was clearly not consulted on important matters, meekly followed, and proceeded to attend to her sister's comforts in the new home.

The tribe accepted the presence of the strangers among them — indeed they had no choice, for the elder sister was not one to tolerate opposition. She spoke but little to her neighbours, who regarded her with a mixture of fear and respect. Not so the younger sister, who was always willing for a merry gossip with the other girls of the village, and soon became a popular member of the group.

"Where do you come from?" the village maidens asked.

"From such a far distance that I do not remember," was the younger sister's reply.

"By what name are you known?"

"That of the Nameless Ones," said the younger sister.

"And what is contained in the great basket belonging to your sister?" This was what had really aroused the girls' curiosity, so they asked it last of all. But the younger sister only answered:

"This you must ask of my sister herself, for certainly I do not know." Indeed she did not, and would dearly have loved to find out. Not one of the maidens cared to approach the Old One, as they had named the elder sister, for they were convinced that she was a witch, and that the basket was more than likely filled to the brim with wicked spells.

"Take care she does not turn you into a witch also," they warned the Young One, who merely laughed enchantingly, and assured them that she knew nothing at all of witchcraft. However she agreed to try and discover her sister's secret. That night when the Young One and the Old One were alone, except for whatever or whoever was con-

tained in that mysterious basket, the Young One said: "Sister, I have followed by your side since I was a small child, and never have I asked of you a single question."

"Ask freely," said the Old One curtly. "Do not however expect a free answer, for I am not obliged to give it."

"Only tell me," begged the Young One, "what is inside that huge basket that you carry. Surely some great treasure, for you do not let it out of your sight, either by day or by night." In fact she had observed that her sister actually slept with one eye open and the other closed, in order to survey the basket.

"Undo the lid of that basket, and you may find yourself undone!" warned the Old One. "Take care that you seek not what is not yours to find." With this recommendation she signified that the conversation had reached an end, and settling down close by the basket, the Old One closed an eye and went to sleep. The Young One, her curiosity still unsatisfied, sat staring at the basket. The more she looked, the more she wondered; and the more she wondered, the more she longed to open the lid and see what it contained.

The next day the village girls gathered round the Young One.

"What news do you bring?" they demanded. "Has the Old One spoken?"

"She has spoken, but told me nothing," the Young One replied ruefully. "And I dare not ask again, for my sister has given me solemn warning never more to mention this matter."

"But we must know what is in the basket. Among us there is talk of nothing else," said the girls.

"I also have much curiosity," admitted the Young One. "And during the long night, a scheme came to my mind, whereby this curiosity shall be satisfied." She would tell them no more of her plan however, but promised that, before another day dawned, the secret of the basket should be solved.

Accordingly the Young One awaited a chance to put her plan into action. As it happened an opportunity occurred that very afternoon, when the Old One called her sister to her side:

"I am going into the forest to gather herbs," she said.

"It is well, sister," replied the Young One, delighted at the prospect of being left alone at last with the basket. "I shall remain to prepare

a succulent meal for your return."

"Come with me, and come now," said the Old One sharply. "For I have no taste for food unseasoned by herbs." The Young One was obliged to accompany her sister to the forest, but she still intended to find out, once and for all, what that basket contained. Wandering a little way ahead of the Old One, the crafty girl suddenly flung herself head-first down in the undergrowth, letting forth piercing shrieks. The Old One came rapidly to the spot and leaned over the Young One anxiously. "What has happened, child?" she demanded. "Speak to your old sister! I would not have you harmed for all the world." The Young One buried her head in her arms, a little guilty about her ruse which seemed to have deceived her sister so successfully. However the plan had been started, and should now go forward. "An enormous forest animal flung itself at my back and knocked me down," she gasped. "The shock was great, and I must go home to recover." The Old One could only see one or two innocent little birds in the area, which was far from the river where the deadly crocodiles lived, and the kangaroos were way out on the plain. Even so, it seemed clear that the Young One had received a bad fright, and the Old One, who was in reality more gentle than she appeared, and loved her sister, said: "Go back then child to our home, and await my return." The Young One needed no encouragement. With much alacrity for one supposed to have been hurt, she jumped up and ran all the way back to the hut, where the basket, for once, lay un-attended. At last the great opportunity had arrived. With trembling

fingers the Young One undid the woven strap and peeped into the interior of the basket, where *something* stirred. Amazed at her own temerity, the Young One daringly raised the lid still further, and then dropped it again with a shriek that was this time quite genuine. For her gaze had met the beady stare of a hooded serpent, who reared upwards out of the basket, hissing dangerously at her. The Young One stood transfixed with horror as the serpent slowly and deliberately uncoiled yard after yard after yard of itself, slithering silently across the floor of the hut and out into the world. The Young One gathered her wits and tried to catch hold of the fast disappearing tail, but the serpent had already burrowed a hole in the ground, and was gradually sliding into it.

"Come back!" cried the girl in dismay, but the serpent's tail gave a derisive flick and vanished completely into the earth. Now the Young One was really distressed, for she had lost her sister's most prized possession. She must go at once to the Old One and confess the whole story of her deception. The Young One went speedily back along the route to the forest, and beneath her running feet the ground rumbled and shook, as the serpent tunnelled along under the earth. Soon the Young One was obliged to slow her pace, for the ground was unaccountably becoming muddy. Water rose up ahead of her, drowning the bushes in a swirling stream. The stream became a great river, and on the opposite bank the Young One saw her sister, unable to

get across. Because of her unforgivable behaviour, the sisters, who had never been apart, would now be forever parted. The Young One began to cry miserably, and her tears were as profuse as the rain. But the Old One raised both her arms upwards and cried: "Serpent, master of the water, rise and carry me home!"

From the oozing ground in front of the Young One emerged the head of the giant serpent. Up came yard after yard of wriggling snake, rearing high over the river, until it met the opposite bank, where the Old One waited. There came a noise like the rumbling of thunder, and the Young One realized it sounded from somewhere within the interior of the giant serpent. "Climb upon my back, Old One," the serpent roared. And the Old One, stepping carefully in the wide-patterned ridges of the snake's skin, which spanned the river from bank to bank, went across the serpent bridge and rejoined her sister on the other side.

"This is your doing, my girl." She spoke severely, but embraced the Young One fondly, nevertheless. "See, you have released the master of the water, whom I have guarded carefully all these years, in order to save the earth from floods. Now we may all be drowned; for wherever the serpent goes, the waters must gather." Indeed at that very moment it began to rain. But the sonorous voice of the serpent spoke again: "You, who have nurtured and tended me this long time shall not perish in a flood. I, master of the waters, who for so long lay hidden in the depths of a basket, shall now rise to take my rightful place in the heavens. You may bid me farewell, Old One; but expect to see me again, whenever the rain and the sun hold truce."

As his last words echoed and died, the sun appeared from behind a raincloud and cast a watery beam downwards towards the river. With a wave of his tail the serpent slowly began to disappear. Now the rain fell and the sun shone; and the two sisters standing together saw that a huge bright rainbow spanned the river, where once the serpent's body had stretched from bank to bank.

And that was how the rainbow came, as it does until this very day, when the sun and the rain unite.

TALE OF THE DOG-STAR

Bungil, the revered chief of the Ganawarra tribe, had always longed for a son who would one day take his place. When, after some years, a baby boy was at last born to him, the chief could hardly contain his joy. "My son shall grow tall as a sapling. His thoughts shall be curved and flexible as the boomerang, his feet as nimble as the kangaroo. As a wise chief shall he speak to you words of peace and good council – all this do I promise my people for Binbeal, son of Bungil!"

To be sure the baby was fine and sturdy enough; bright-eyed as a bird, and brave enough not to cry under any circumstances. But even so, sad to tell, the little Binbeal was unable to fulfil his father's hopes. For long after all the other babies of his own age had learned to talk, Binbeal could not say a single word.

Anxiously his father pointed out each of the objects with which Binbeal was familiar, and spoke their names. "Tree," he said. "Flower." And the small fellow would toddle towards the tree and touch it, or pick a flower from the bush, in order to show that he understood. Yet he could never repeat the words after his father, no matter how hard he tried.

Here indeed was a tragedy. If Binbeal had been a little boy living nowadays, nobody would have blamed him for his inability to speak. On the contrary, kind teachers would show him the way to make himself understood; and before long he might have been able to read and write and even talk as well as any other child. In those far-off days, however, and in that part of the world, the people believed that a child who could not speak must be bewitched. And when this misfortune happened to a son of their chief, the tribe could only think that some great evil had been visited upon them, and that they would all be made to suffer for it.

Accordingly one day when Binbeal was scarcely four years old, a deputation of elders visited Bungil, "Good chief," they said, "far be it that our people should wish to harm their leader, or that which belongs to him. Yet there is much fear among us that this child who makes no sound, he who will one day be our chief, has been sent by the wicked spirits in order to punish us. For the good of all we must ask that you sacrifice your son, that these spirits may be appeased." In vain did the chief, who did not think as they did, try to explain that his son's silence was no sign of misfortune. He, proud soul, even fell on his knees to plead for the life of the little boy. But the elders were afraid, and in their terror they were without pity.

"Go to the forest, and make an end of this child who has brought the displeasure of the gods to our tribe." Brave and strong as he was, the chief was but one man against many. Seeing that they would kill Binbeal there and then if he refused, Bungil carried the child sorrowfully away to the woods. The forest stopped short on the edge of a hilly incline, at the bottom of which was a beach. Bungil took his baby son right down to the shore and sat him on a small rock. Soon the tide would come in and cover the rock. Little Binbeal, the son of his hopes and dreams, would be drowned. What other alternative was there, except to leave the little boy to starve to death in the forest?

Little Binbeal smiled trustingly up at his father. How could a baby be expected to understand that he must be punished for a fault that was not his? Bungil thought that his heart would burst in sorrow for the dreadful deed he must do.

Just then a voice sounded unexpectedly behind him. "This child shall not be harmed," it said. Bungil swung round, but could see nobody. Only a lean dog stood gently pawing the sand. "Yes, it is I who speak," said the dog, to Bungil's astonishment. "Rest assured that your son will be safe with me. Go back to your tribe now, and visit us from time to time. You shall find that all is well with this fine young warrior!" The dog wagged his tail so merrily that the baby chuckled contentedly and held out his fat arms towards the animal. The dog approached, picked the child up in a velvety soft mouth, and set him astride his back. Then he trotted off towards the woods, leaving Bungil, to return to his people, suddenly light-hearted.

"Have you rid us of the dumb one, and so diverted from your people the wrath of the gods?" they demanded.

"You shall not see the child again," said Bungil. For he certainly did not intend that they should. And from this remark the people concluded that Bungil had indeed killed the little boy. Satisfied that they were no longer in danger, and that their chief had taken the correct steps to protect them, Bungil was accepted once more as their leader.

Meanwhile, back in the forest little Binbeal was being well attended. The faithful hound dug him a sheltered hole in the ground, filled it with soft moss and made a canopy of twigs and leaves above, to shelter the child from rain and sun. Each day the dog went hunting, and returned with enough food to provide the baby with all he needed, in order to grow big and strong. Soon the little fellow learned to fend for himself too, under the dog's patient tuition. He could even swim – with a dog-paddle stroke.

Whenever possible Bungil stole away from the tribe to see his son. How delighted he was to find that Binbeal was happy and thriving! His gratitude to the dog was tremendous, but the good animal would accept little credit. "Your son becomes a fine man, for such is his father whom he resembles," the dog would say. Indeed, as the years passed Binbeal became all that his father had desired for him. He was tall, and strong and clever too, even if he was not able to express his intelligence in words. He said a good deal without ever actually speaking. To clasp his father's hand firmly was a good enough way to say that Binbeal felt pleased to see him. And the affection with which he stroked his good friend the dog, said more clearly than any words:

"I shall always be in your debt, faithful hound." Though he was now grown up, Binbeal did not scorn to hug the dear dog as lovingly as he had done as a small child.

It happened one day that an inquisitive woman – such as can be found in most tribes – followed Bungil into the forest on one of his excursions to visit his son. She had often noticed him quietly slipping away, and suspected the chief had a store of food hidden in the forest, which he did not feel disposed to share with the others. The chief, not suspecting that he was being watched, greeted Binbeal and the dog with his usual warmth. The lurking woman yearned to know the identity of the handsome young man who seemed on familiar terms with the chief. Could he possibly be the son whom Bungil had promised to kill, so many years ago? And did her ears deceive her, or could the hound, standing nearby, actually speak?

What witchcraft was this? A son who could utter no word at all, and a dog who spoke with the tongue of man? No doubt of it. The chief had been deceiving them all along and must himself be in league with the bad spirits!

The woman fled back to the village, eager to impart this awful news to the elders.

But the dog, with his sensitive nose, had detected the presence of a stranger. "Your son is in danger," he warned the chief. "Return to the village and try to placate your people, for they have discovered that Binbeal lives."

The chief hastened back, and the dog turned to the young man. "Now listen well, and obey my words exactly, for this may be the last I shall speak," he said. "I fear that your father may not be able to stay the anger of the men of the tribe. They will come, despite his efforts, and in their terror, they will try to kill you. But you, who were born to lead men into wiser paths, must protect yourself. And this is the way. Take this axe which you yourself have made, and with one blow strike me down."

"This I cannot obey," exclaimed the young man. 'How should I harm my faithful friend, whom I love dearly?"

"You will only seem to hurt me," said the dog. "I am the spirit of your lost voice, which was found in the forest the day you were born. When I go back to the heavens, you will find your voice again; you will speak words of peace and good

54

council, even as your father once promised the people. And so shall they learn the error of their ways, and believe not in the powers of evil, but in the powers of good! Now heed this. After I am gone you shall burn my body, and rub yourself with the ashes. These will protect you from injury, so that no mortal man can harm you. Now, perform your task at once, and weep not, for I shall feel nothing."

Sick at heart, but realizing that the time had come to part with his loyal friend, Binbeal struck a blow at the dog, who fell dead instantly.

Mournfully the young man set about obeying the dog's last

commands. Building a fire, he reduced the body to ashes, with which he covered himself. Then, in an attempt to wash away his misery. Binbeal dived into the sea and swam about vigorously.

Back at the village, the woman soon gathered together a group of excited folk, who were fast joined by the elders.

"What is this you say of dogs with the voice of man, and of man with no voice?" they demanded. "Such talk is but of dreams in the mind of a foolish woman."

"I doubt not what I see with my own eyes, and hear with my own ears!" exclaimed the woman.

"It is known her ears are sharp enough to hear any manner of strange things," commented one of the men. "And her tongue longer still, for she is ever stretching it!"

"You would speak less lightly did you suspect what I myself know," said the woman indignantly.

"And what knowledge has this

woman that we, the elders do not possess?'' asked one of the wise men.

"At the least I can tell true from false!" retorted the woman. "It is true that the son of the chief is alive, and who would prove it false must accompany me to the edge of the forest."

"Here is the chief, let him answer for this," shouted the villagers.

The chief could see at once that the woman had revealed his secret to everyone.

"What truth is there," said one of the elders, "that your son, whom you promised to kill, remains alive? Have you thus deceived us, in all these years, and placed the whole village in danger of destruction by the avenging spirits?"

"My people, it is true I have indeed deceived you. But only for the sake of a poor harmless child.

"Harmless indeed. The spirits who made the child speechless, they will harm *us*!" shouted the woman. "If you value your lives and those of your wives and children, the silent one must die!"

"He has grown into a fine young man. I beg you, let him live, and perhaps one day, in spite of his silence, he may yet be a credit to our tribe," pleaded the chief. But the people were mad with fear. "Take us to the place where the silent one dwells," they screamed. "We must do what should have been done these many years!"

The woman, proud of the sensation she had caused, and of the important role she was now called upon to play, led the way back

through the forest towards the beach. The chief followed, ever begging his people to show mercy, but they would not listen.

At last they approached the beach, and gathered together pointing excitedly, as a young man swam towards them with wide strokes. Emerging from the sea he stood in the sun, the water dripping from his splendid shining body, like some heavenly god-like creature.

"There he is!" called the woman who had led them there, triumphantly. "See how his face resembles that of the chief. Who now will believe not that there stands the son of our leader?"

The men approached in a threatening group, and stood before the young man, who did not flinch. "Are you Binbeal, son of Bungil, our chief?" they demanded.

The young man nodded his head.

"The same who was struck dumb by the spirits, and now must die to appease them?" said the men. "Harbinger of misfortune, you should long ago have died. Now prepare to meet your end."

"Rather take my life," protested the chief. "After all, it was I who first deceived you."

"Would you then perish also?" cried the men, in a frenzy of terror. "Do the gods demand this of us too?" They were actually prepared to raise their weapons against the good man, who had led them so wisely and well. The chief made no attempt to defend himself, such was his despair. But Binbeal did. Dashing between the sharp blades

that were ready to strike down his father, he received the blows himself. Yet to the astonishment of the attackers, their knives and axes rebounded from the young man's body, leaving no mark.

"Truly the speechless one is bewitched!" cried the men in dismay. "We cannot harm him"

"And neither shall you!" spoke a voice, and it was the voice of Binbeal, who had been called the silent one. "Know that I am speechless no longer. Hear, all cowards and wrong-doers that I, the son of your chief, am no man bewitched. My tongue is as your tongue, but more bold and more honest.

"You, not I, do seek to believe in evil, and shall bring evil to your-selves. The killing of innocents cannot bring protection from harm. My voice, which I have newly found, shall speak to you words of peace and good council, even as my father promised."

The chief could hardly believe his ears. Not only had his son found his voice, but it was the voice of authority with which he spoke!

"My son, you have brought much honour to your old father, and to our tribe," he said. "Now they may see that Binbeal, son of Bungil, is blessed of the gods.

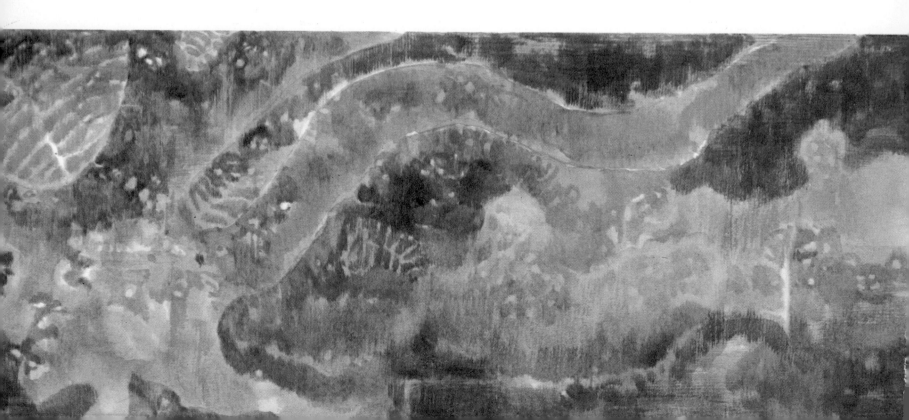

"Blessed! Our tribe is blessed of the gods!" cried the people. "We no longer fear their anger, for surely if the silent one speaks, it is a propitious sign"

Undoubtedly a miracle had occurred, for the people took courage themselves from the brave words of father and son. No longer did they shake with terror at the thought of angering the bad spirits, when a child was born without as much ability as the next.

The chief led the tribe until he was old and infirm, and later it was Binbeal who carried the weight and responsibility of his people's welfare. He spoke, as his father had promised long ago when he was born, with words of peace and good council.

When there was uncertainty in his mind how to administer justice in a way which was kind and right at the same time, Binbeal would stand at night outside his hut, and look up at the sky. Twinkling down at him knowingly was the dog-star, which had made its appearance in the heavens, the very day that the faithful hound had died. And then there were no more doubts.